NORMAN BRIDWELL

P9-CEX-728

Clifford GROWS UP

SCHOLASTIC INC.
New York Toronto London Auckland Sydney

Clifford the Small Red Puppy ©1972, 1985 by Norman Bridwell, **Clifford's Family** ©1984 by Norman Bridwell, **Clifford's First Autumn** ©1997 by Norman Bridwell, **Clifford's First Christmas** ©1994 by Norman Bridwell, **Clifford's First Halloween** ©1995 by Norman Bridwell, **Clifford's First Snow Day** ©1998 by Norman Bridwell, **Clifford's First Valentine's Day** ©1997 by Norman Bridwell, and **Clifford's First Puppy Days** ©1989 by Norman Bridwell. All published by Scholastic Inc.

No part of this publication may be reproduced in whole or in part, or stored in a retrieval system, or transmitted in any form or by any means, electronic, mechanical, photocopying, recording, or otherwise, without written permission of the publisher. For information regarding permissions, write to Scholastic Inc., Attention: Permissions Department, 555 Broadway, New York, NY 10012.

ISBN 0-439-08233-1

Compilation copyright © 1999 by Norman Bridwell.
All rights reserved. Published by Scholastic Inc.
SCHOLASTIC, CARTWHEEL BOOKS, and associated logos are trademarks
and/or registered trademarks of Scholastic Inc.
CLIFFORD, CLIFFORD THE SMALL RED PUPPY, and CLIFFORD THE BIG RED DOG and associated logos
are trademarks and/or trademarks of Norman Bridwell.

10 9 8 7

0/0 01 02 03 04

Printed in the U.S.A.
First printing, April 1999

Hi! I'm Emily Elizabeth and
I want to show you some special
pictures of my dog Clifford.
You'll notice that he has grown up a lot!

When Clifford was a puppy,
he was so tiny that I had to
feed him with my doll's bottle.

And he was so small that I could
dress him up in my doll's clothes.

He was just the right size for my electric toy car.

And he liked to hide in my dollhouse.

But I had to be careful when
I played with Clifford.

Even the smallest collar I could find was too big for him.

And when he began to eat dog food, I had to watch him all the time.

My puppy's first snow day
was a big adventure.

Here is a picture of a snowman I made with my friend.
I wanted Clifford to be in the picture, too.
Do you know what?

He was!

Clifford was always getting lost.
One time, he got lost at the post office.
Can you see my small red puppy?

Everyone cheered when we found him!

Here I was making valentines.

Clifford made one, too!

When summer came, Clifford chased birds.

But he never caught one.

In autumn, Clifford chased falling leaves.
He had fun!

In this picture, Clifford was playing football.

Clifford even scored a touchdown!

On Halloween, Clifford liked
the Jack-o'-lantern.

Clifford was the littlest ghost
I had ever seen.

That Halloween, Clifford discovered candy apples.

The candy was sort of sticky!

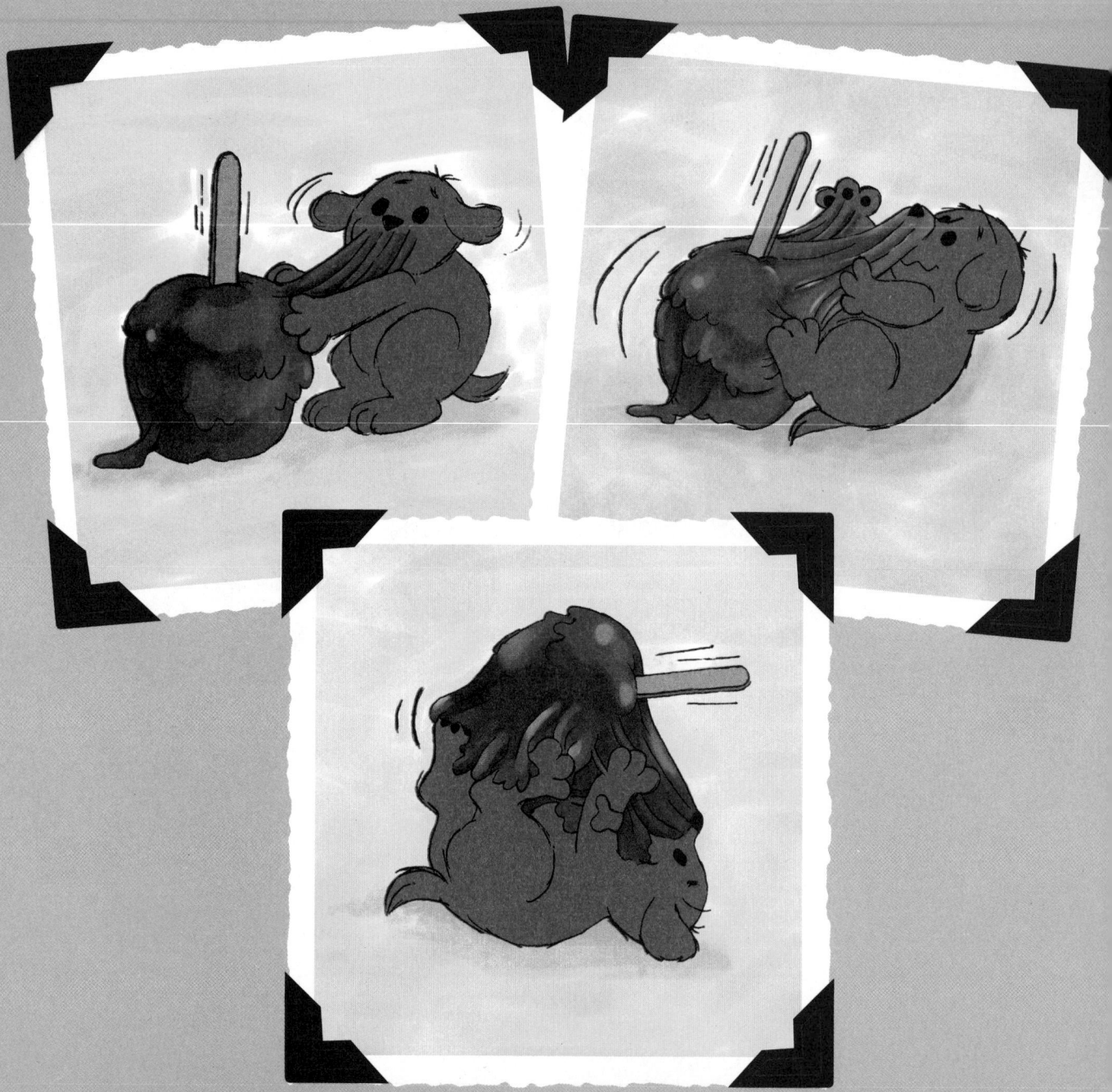

Before Christmas, Clifford helped me wrap presents.

Clifford's first present from Santa was a bone.

For the new year, we had a wonderful surprise.
Clifford began to grow.

He grew some more.

And he grew some more.

We had to move from the city to the country.
This picture shows Clifford on moving day.

And this is Clifford all grown up.

I love my big red dog!

Look for the pictures from

Clifford Grows Up

in these other funny books.

Clifford's Puppy Days

Clifford The Small Red Puppy

Clifford's First Christmas

Clifford's First Snow Day

Clifford's First Valentine's Day

Clifford's First Autumn

Clifford's First Halloween

Clifford's Family

Happy Reading!